To my shadow

MEET THE

Cinnabar

NAME:
Helen Michaels

FAIRY NAME AND SPIRIT:
Cinnabar

WAND:
An Aspen Twig

GIFT:
Enhanced abilities at night

MENTOR:
Mrs. Thompson,
Madam Finch

Spiderwort

NAME:
Jensen Fortini

FAIRY NAME AND SPIRIT:
Spiderwort

WAND:
Small, Brilliant Red
Cardinal Feather

GIFT:
Cleverness; the ability to come up
with good ideas and plans

MENTOR:
Godmother,
Madam Chameleon

Cinnabar

and
the Island of Shadows

J. H. Sweet

Illustrated by Holly Sierra

SOURCEBOOKS
Jabberwocky
AN IMPRINT OF SOURCEBOOKS

Published by Sourcebooks Jabberwocky, an imprint of Sourcebooks, Inc.
P.O. Box 4410, Naperville, Illinois 60567-4410
(630) 961-3900
Fax: (630) 961-2168
www.sourcebooks.com

Library of Congress Cataloging-in-Publication Data

Sweet, J. H.
  Cinnabar and the Island of Shadows / J.H. Sweet.
      p. cm.
  "The Fairy Chronicles."
  Summary: When seven children are born without their shadows, Cinnabar and her fairy friends must travel to the Island of Shadows to find out who has taken them.
  ISBN-13: 978-1-4022-1161-4 (pbk.)
  ISBN-10: 1-4022-1161-9 (pbk.)
  [1. Fairies—Fiction. 2. Magic—Fiction. 3. Shadows—Fiction.] I. Title.
  PZ7.S9547Ci 2008
  [Fic]—dc22
                                                   2007037137

Printed and bound in the United States of America
IN 10 9 8 7 6 5 4 3 2 1

FAIRY TEAM

Mimosa

NAME:
Alexandra Hastings

FAIRY NAME AND SPIRIT:
Mimosa

WAND:
Emu Feather

GIFT:
Sensitive and understanding of
others' needs

MENTOR:
Evelyn Holstrom,
Madam Monarch

Dewberry

NAME:
Lauren Kelley

FAIRY NAME AND SPIRIT:
Dewberry

WAND:
Single Strand of Braided
Unicorn Tail Hair

GIFT:
Great knowledge and wisdom

MENTOR:
Grandmother,
Madam Goldenrod

Inside you is the power to do anything

The Fairy Chronicles

Come visit us at fairychronicles.com

Contents

Chapter One

Cinnabar

The early morning rays of summer sunshine were just beginning to slant through the bedroom windows. Helen Michaels had been awake for nearly two hours already, practicing ballet. Helen was a thin, willowy black girl with delicate features and straight dark hair that fell to just above her shoulders. She liked to keep her hair fairly short because it was easy to tie back into a small bun during ballet practices and performances.

At ten years old, Helen had already been studying ballet for four years. When her parents realized how serious she was about it, and recognized her talent, they had installed mirrors and bars along one wall of her large bedroom. Helen attended ballet lessons three times a week. If her dance skills continued to progress as expected, she was planning, at age twelve, to attend a special school for the arts, rather than public school.

Helen's mother was an artist who concentrated on oil paintings. Mrs. Michaels sold her work through several art galleries in the region. Helen's father was a doctor who specialized in feet, a podiatrist. Helen knew she was very lucky that her parents were able to send her to ballet classes. Some children's parents couldn't afford to do this. And since she enjoyed dancing very much, she didn't waste the opportunity. She worked hard every day to improve her skills.

Her best practice sessions occurred late at night and early in the morning, and there was a special reason for this. In addition to

being a regular girl, Helen was also a fairy. At birth, she had been given the fairy spirit of a cinnabar moth. When Cinnabar was nine years old, her fairy mentor told her about the fairy spirit and began teaching her everything she needed to know about being a fairy.

Mentors were usually older fairies, assigned to help younger fairies learn about fairy things. Being a fairy was a tremendous responsibility, so mentors were also given the task of teaching young fairies not to abuse their power and not to use fairy magic for trivial matters.

Cinnabar's mentor was her ballet instructor, Mrs. Thompson, who had been given a finch fairy spirit. Madam Finch taught Cinnabar the purpose of fairies. She also instructed her on how to use the fairy handbook, pixie dust, and her wand.

Madam Finch was often able to arrange for Cinnabar to spend time away from home to participate in fairy activities. When Madam Finch and Cinnabar were engaged in fairy adventures, Cinnabar's parents usually thought they were going to ballet workshops or attending out-of-town performances. Sometimes, sleepovers with friends were arranged so that Cinnabar could go on fairy missions.

Fairies were given the job of protecting nature and fixing serious problems, mainly problems caused by the mischief and mayhem of other magical creatures. As terrific problem solvers, fairies were often called upon to help others.

The fairy handbook gave answers to fairy questions, and guided fairies to make good decisions. Cinnabar carried her handbook on her belt, along with a tiny pouch of glittering magical pixie dust, which was needed for various fairy spells.

Cinnabar carried an enchanted aspen twig for her wand. The twig was a creamy gray-and-white color. Fairy wands were very diverse and could be made from almost anything. The aspen twig was very simple compared to many fairy wands. But Cinnabar was extremely happy with it. Aspen trees stood for quiet strength and solitude, and this suited the reserved nature of her personality perfectly.

When Cinnabar met with her fellow fairies at Fairy Circles, the girls often compared fairy wands. The vast variety of wands included many types of feathers such as pheasant, cardinal, mockingbird, raven, ostrich, bluebird, peacock, and emu. There were also a lot of flower wands like tulips, miniature roses, poppies, and clover blossoms. Some of the more unique wands included a porcupine quill, a thin crystal shard, an elephant's eyelash, braided orangutan hairs, a dandelion seed, a corkscrew-spiraled boar bristle, and a pussy willow branch. There were also wands made from sprigs of mistletoe, gleaming pieces of golden straw, pine needles, and polished wood splinters like mahogany, pecan, and silver birch. Madam Finch carried a very powerful wand that was made from a tiger's whisker. But Cinnabar wouldn't have traded her wand for any of the fancier ones. She loved her aspen twig.

Standard fairy form was six inches high. As a fairy, Cinnabar wore a dress made of black velvet fuzz that came to just above her knees; and she had tall, brilliant red wings with sooty gray striping along the edges. She also wore a black velvet belt and matching slippers. Cinnabar was the most graceful and coordinated of all the fairies. And even though she was somewhat shy, she drew attention with her poise and beauty.

Fairies were given special gifts relating to their fairy spirits. As her special fairy gift, Cinnabar was given the ability to perform well at night. She had more energy and could see better and fly better during the nighttime.

In fairy form, Madam Finch wore a delicate, billowing, greenish-yellow dress made of tiny furry finch feathers. The dress fell almost to her ankles, and she wore soft slippers to match. Madam Finch was tall, with short blond hair and bright, feathery green wings. Since finches were very good-natured and agreeable birds, her special fairy gift was the ability to get along well with anyone. She was often able to help smooth over tensions and settle disputes. And as one of the most even-tempered fairies, she could help calm down heated situations when needed.

Cinnabar was very excited this morning because she and Madam Finch would be attending a Fairy Circle later in the day. Madam Finch had also arranged for a two-night sleepover at another fairy's home so

that Cinnabar could participate in a very important fairy mission. Since there were still three more weeks of summer vacation left, there was plenty of time for fairy activities.

While Cinnabar was practicing ballet, a squirrel delivered a nut message to her window ledge. (Nut messages were hollowed-out nuts used as vessels for fairy notes and letters.) Madam Finch had sent the pecan this morning to inform Cinnabar that she would be picking her up at nine o'clock, and that everything had been arranged with her parents with regards to the sleepover. Madam Finch also wanted to let Cinnabar know that there would be two new moth fairies at the Fairy Circle, whose spirits were those of a cisthene moth and a luna moth.

The last part of the message was especially exciting news for Cinnabar. So far, she had been the only moth fairy at Fairy Circle. There were a lot of butterfly fairies in the region, along with various other insect fairies including a firefly, a dragonfly, and a June beetle; but so far, there had not been any other moth fairies. A dewberry fairy and a goldenrod fairy would also be joining their group for the first time at Fairy Circle.

Cinnabar took a shower and changed clothes in a hurry; then she quickly packed her overnight bag and rushed to have a bowl of cereal for breakfast. She was very anxious for Madam Finch to arrive.

Chapter Two

$\mathcal{F}$airy $\mathcal{C}$ircle

Madam Finch arrived promptly at
nine o'clock, and they set off right
away in her blue sedan. They stopped once
along the way to pick up another fairy.
Jensen Fortini was a spiderwort herb fairy.
Spiderwort's neighbor, Bailey Richardson,
was a rosemary fairy. However, Rosemary
was traveling with her family on a summer
trip, so she wouldn't be attending today's
Fairy Circle meeting.

In fairy form, Spiderwort wore a dark
green dress made of long, pointy leaves with
bright blue flowers scattered over the bodice

and skirt. The blue flowers had lovely, spindly, bright yellow centers. Spiderwort also had tall blue wings and short, strawberry blond hair, pulled back into a headband covered with tiny spiderwort flowers. Her wand was a bright red cardinal feather, and her special fairy gift involved cleverness and quick thinking. She was a terrific problem solver and could come up with answers and good plans faster than any other fairy. Spiderwort was also very organized and thorough. She was good at chess and was already studying debate, which was somewhat unusual for a ten-year-old.

Spiderwort had heard about the new fairies from her mentor, Madam Chameleon, and was also very excited about the upcoming fairy gathering.

They only had to travel about fifteen minutes to reach a secluded park on the outskirts of town. Today, the fairies were meeting under a bald cypress tree on the edge of a small pond. Madam Toad, the leader of the fairies, always chose their Fairy Circle sites with great care. They usually met under trees with special meaning, which often related to the purpose of their pending fairy mission. As she parked the car, Madam Finch explained that cypress trees were symbolic of darkness, shadows, and mourning.

By the time Cinnabar, Spiderwort, and Madam Finch arrived, about twenty fairies were already flitting around the base of the tree. A few of them were sitting on the knobby knees of the bald cypress, which were actually some of the tree's roots sticking straight up out of the water's edge.

As the girls joined their friends, Cinnabar and Spiderwort noticed that Madam Toad was engaged in a discussion with a very tired-looking elf. The elf was barely two feet high, had dark hair, and was dressed in a green shirt with brown pants.

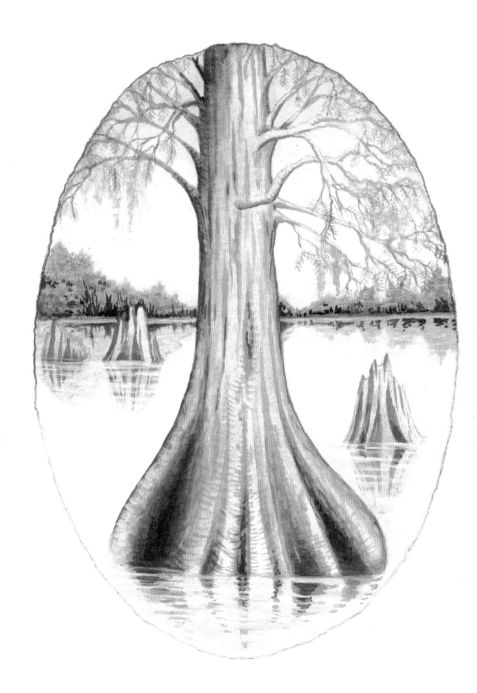

Elves were very old magical creatures, even though they looked young. And they never aged or died because they were immortal. Elves also had very powerful magic that was largely unknown to other magical creatures. They did not wear pointy shoes, and barely had the smallest of points on the tips of their ears, so they never looked like elves in storybooks.

Brownie Christopher, the leader of the brownies, was also present, standing next to Madam Toad and the elf. Brownies were boy fairies, about seven inches high, who got their fairy spirits from things such as mosses, turquoise, slate, clover, amber, granite, quartz, pinecones, and river stones. They couldn't fly like girl fairies, but often used animals and birds to help them travel.

Christopher was an acorn brownie with dark hair. He was dressed in soft tan clothes and wore an acorn cap for a hat.

The brownie leader looked almost as tired as the elf.

At one point, when Cinnabar was by herself for a moment, Christopher approached her and slipped a small acorn into her hand. "This is from James," he said gruffly. He turned away quickly as Cinnabar blushed a bright crimson, with her face and neck becoming almost as red as her wings.

Cinnabar had met Brownie James earlier this summer while seeking out the missing Princess of Haiku. He had also participated in the challenge to recharge the Cave of Courage. James and Cinnabar liked each other very much and had been corresponding with one another through nut messages. The nut held a tiny white flower—a baby's breath. She tucked the flower into her belt. The delicate blossom was a beautiful contrast to her black dress.

Cinnabar and Spiderwort flew around the Fairy Circle, greeting many of their friends including Firefly, Morning Glory, Thistle, Marigold, Dragonfly, Mimosa, Primrose, and Hollyhock.

Hollyhock was the only deaf fairy of their group; and her cousin, Primrose, was using sign language to interpret for her. Madam Swallowtail was Hollyhock's mentor and also knew sign language. And many of the fairies were taking American Sign Language classes at the local community college.

There was a great deal of excitement among the fairies about meeting the newcomers because Dewberry and Madam Goldenrod had already arrived.

Dewberry's real name was Lauren Kelley. She wore a green dress of creeping vines with tiny black dewberries nestled among the leaves. Her short, wavy hair was nearly as black as her berries. Dewberry's small wings were a soft, misty green color; and her wand was a single strand of braided unicorn tail hair that glistened brightly and was white as snow.

Madam Goldenrod, Dewberry's grandmother and mentor, had searched an apple orchard over and over again for nearly two weeks to find the unicorn hair. Unicorns were drawn to apple trees, but it was very rare to see a unicorn, and Madam Goldenrod wasn't even sure that any had ever visited that particular orchard. However, after careful and persistent searching, she had gotten lucky.

Dewberry was given the special fairy gift of great wisdom and knowledge, which made her something like an encyclopedia with common sense. She processed information very quickly and had a correct answer for almost every question. Dewberry also knew about legends, as well as facts.

Madam Goldenrod's name was Beverly Kelley. Her silvery white hair was short and wavy, and her dress was a golden sunset color with a satiny glow. She had tall, autumn gold wings and carried a tiny hummingbird feather for her wand. The feather was the smallest wand any of the fairies had ever seen, and was dark green in color with a slight turquoise and purple sheen. Madam Goldenrod's special fairy gift was good sense and precaution, with the ability to sense danger and deception. She also had the power to force others to tell the truth, if necessary.

Cinnabar happily made her way across the Fairy Circle to greet the two new moth fairies when they arrived. Luna had pale green wings with luminous eyespots and soft pink edges. Cisthene's wings were divided into gray, peach, and pink sections. Both of the new moth fairies were very beautiful and captured everyone's attention.

On the other side of the circle, Spiderwort was visiting with her friend, Mimosa. Mimosa's real name was Alexandra Hastings. She had long, straight blond hair that

gleamed almost as brightly as her glistening dress made of thin mimosa flower strands in colors of peach, light pink, white, and dark pink. Her pale pink wings were very tall and wispy, and she carried an emu feather wand that was curled on its forked ends. Mimosa also smelled like fresh, ripe peaches. Everyone around her breathed deeply to take in the wonderfully fresh and fruity smell.

Mimosa's unique fairy gift was the ability to be exceptionally sensitive and caring of others. She was intuitive, understanding of others' needs, and a good advisor. At age ten, she already knew that she wanted to be a professional counselor when she grew up—either a school counselor or a therapist. She hadn't decided which yet.

The fairies continued to visit with the new members of their group while enjoying refreshments of raspberries, cherry chip loaf, homemade fudge, powdered sugar puff pastries, lemon jellybeans, peanut butter and marshmallow crème sandwiches, pomegranate juice, and root beer.

After about thirty minutes of visiting, Madam Toad called the meeting to order.

Chapter Three

*S*hadows and Shadowmakers

adam Toad had been the leader of the Southwest region of fairies for a very long time. She was the oldest and wisest fairy, and her voice was very deep and loud. The fairy leader was rather plump with tiny green wings and a shimmering, pale green dress laden with moisture drops. She carried a miniature red rosebud-stem wand and wore a crown of tiny red rosebuds to match.

The elf and Christopher sat to one side of Madam Toad and listened politely as she began to speak. Madam Swallowtail stood a little to one side of the group, near

Hollyhock, to interpret for her. Sign language was so graceful and beautiful that the fairies often ended up watching Madam Swallowtail or Primrose, while they were signing, instead of focusing on Madam Toad.

"Welcome! Welcome!" Madam Toad began. "And especially welcome to our new fairies—Dewberry, Luna, Cisthene, and Madam Goldenrod. We are very happy to have you join our group."

There was applause, and Madam Toad paused before she continued. "There is a very serious problem we need to discuss, but I must give you a little background information and some details before we get to that. Some of you may already know why human beings have a shadow. If this is the case, please bear with me while I explain to the others.

"Human shadows are unlike any other shadows on earth. They are much different than animal, mountain, plant, cloud, insect, and building shadows. For starters, human shadows are much more complex. And they are the only shadows that are magically constructed. Human shadows are manufactured by shadowmakers on the Island of Shadows, and are delivered to children shortly after their births by hawks that work for the shadowmakers."

This was indeed new information for most of the young fairies, and they all listened attentively as Madam Toad went on. "The purpose of our shadow is threefold. First, our shadow keeps us company when we are alone, so that we will not be too lonely or frightened. Second, it acts as a protector. Our shadow can help as a defense against attack. Fewer assaults on human beings occur during daylight when our shadows are fully awake. More often, attacks happen at night when our shadows traditionally sleep, or are tired and groggy from their daily vigil of protecting us. Finally, our shadow acts as a guide into the hereafter when we die. We cannot make the journey into the beyond without our shadow. It must accompany us. Only the shadow knows the way. We would be lost without it."

The fairies all looked around at one another. None of the younger fairies had known of the reasons for their shadows. Those on the outer edge of the group, who were partially in the sunlight, were looking admiringly at their shadows and marveling at them.

Madam Toad drew their attention again as she continued to speak. "From what I have told you, I am sure you can under-stand why we require our shadows, both in life and when our lives end." She paused for a few moments with everyone watching her closely and waiting anxiously for her to go on. "Mother Nature became aware of a problem and contacted me, but we have very few details."

The fairies all looked at one another apprehensively. Mother Nature was the guardian of magical creatures and the supervisor of all of nature. She was extremely busy and very powerful, and usually only contacted the fairies when there were serious matters to be dealt with. Mother Nature was often in dangerous forms such as flood, sleet, hailstorm, avalanche, and tidal wave. Luckily, each time Madam Toad had met with Mother Nature, the fairy guardian was in a safe form like echo, rainbow, breeze, and sand drift.

Madam Toad went on with her story. "Mother Nature has discovered that seven children in various countries of the world have not received their shadows. There are children in Panama, the Netherlands, Canada, South Africa, the United States, and two in Mexico who are without shadows.

Locations of
children without shadows

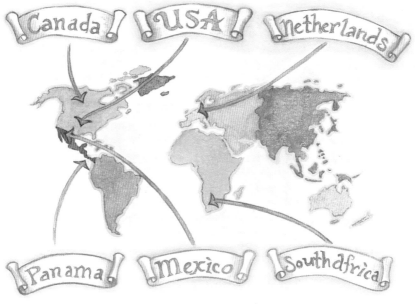

Canada USA Netherlands

Panama Mexico South africa

"At this time," added Madam Toad, "the children are safe. The parents, and other family members, are with the newborns most of the time so they are not lonely or unprotected. And it will be awhile before anyone notices the missing shadows, since tiny babies are not often out in the full sun, and they are not yet crawling or walking to make the absence of a visible shadow obvious.

"However, since we know the importance of our shadows, this problem must be corrected quickly. I have given you all of the details I know about the missing shadows. Since we have little to go on, this mission will be very tricky. The selected group of fairies must travel to the Island of Shadows, meet with the King and Queen of Shadowland, discover what is wrong, and try to fix the problem.

"But there is something very important that you must observe while on the Island of Shadows." Madam Toad paused slightly before going on. "Shadowmakers are forbidden to look upon any shadows they have created after the shadows have been joined with their humans. Looking at a joined-shadow that they have made would be fatal to them. So we must be very careful.

"The island must be approached at night, and you must not let your shadows be seen in moonlight or starlight while you are there. This will be tricky. There is no electricity on the island, and there are no lanterns or candles because the shadow-makers do not need them. But shadows cast by sunlight, moonlight, or starlight could mean death to the residents of the island, so you must all be extremely diligent and careful while you are there."

Next, Madam Toad introduced the elf. "This is Trace. Elf *Travel-Sleep* is the fastest way to get to the West Coast, where you will depart for the Island of Shadows. You will arrive at your coastal point of departure

immediately with the elf travel magic, and it will only take forty-five minutes for you to come out of the *Travel-Sleep-Spell*.

"Brownie Christopher has been working hard with his brownies on the West Coast," Madam Toad continued. "They are seeking out hawks and other birds, in an attempt to contact the hawks that work on the Island of Shadows, so you will have transportation once you reach the coast.

"I have decided that Cinnabar will lead this mission," the fairy leader said. "Her night capabilities will be invaluable. Spiderwort, Mimosa, and Dewberry will accompany her. Madam Finch and Madam Goldenrod will supervise."

Madam Toad smiled a bit as she added, "We are sending our 'thinker' fairies on this mission. Since there is so little to go on, we will need knowledge, wisdom, problem solving, and quick thinking. No fairy has ever met with the King and Queen of

Shadowland, or any of the shadowmakers, before. We will also need sensitivity, understanding, caution, common sense, and caring to effectively interact with them and deal with this problem."

As they were getting ready to leave, Cinnabar looked up Island of Shadows in her fairy handbook. She read the entry aloud to Spiderwort, Dewberry, and Mimosa who were nearby:

"*Island of Shadows*: *The Island of Shadows, sometimes called Shadowland, is located somewhere off the West Coast. Home to the King and Queen of Shadowland, and about five hundred shadowmakers, the island is the source of all human shadows. They are manufactured on the island by the shadowmakers. Shadow manufacture is a complex process, requiring much skill. Each shadow is a different individual, just like the human being it is made for. Shadows are not interchangeable with each other, and the hawks that deliver shadows to humans are specially trained to locate the specific newborn children to whom the shadows belong. The hawks have never yet made a delivery mistake."*

Provisions had already been packed for the fairies in little backpacks and included food, water, pillows, and blankets. The packs were stuffed full of lemon jellybeans, raspberries, and peanut butter and marshmallow crème sandwiches.

The group assembled quickly and said goodbye to their friends, who wished them luck.

While they were waiting for Trace to finish talking to Madam Toad, Cinnabar looked up one more entry in her handbook, and again read aloud:

"*Shadowmakers: These are the beings who construct human shadows. About five hundred shadowmakers inhabit the Island of Shadows. No one has ever seen a shadowmaker, so it is unknown what they look like. The shadowmakers are not standoffish; their isolation is for safety reasons. It is fatal for shadowmakers to look at any shadow they have created, after the shadow has left the island and been united with its human. Although they work on many at one time, it takes approximately six months for a shadowmaker to complete construction of a single human shadow.*"

Chapter Four

The Journey to the Island

race instructed the fairies to close their eyes while he put them under the *Travel-Sleep-Spell.* Almost immediately, the fairies heard the sound of surf and smelled salt water in the air. They awoke to find that they were lying on a lonely stretch of rocky, sandy beach. Trace had watched over them for forty-five minutes until they safely came out of the spell.

The fairies were amazed that elf travel was so instantaneous. They had arrived less than one second after they closed their eyes; but since they didn't remember the

forty-five minute sleep, they were slightly disoriented, looking around for a few moments and rubbing their eyes. As far as they remembered, they had just been at Fairy Circle a moment ago in the shade of the towering bald cypress tree.

The fairies discovered that Christopher's West Coast brownies had been successful in their attempts to contact the shadowmakers' hawks. A large hawk was waiting for them to wake up. Two unknown moss brownies were just departing on the back of a spotted owl. They gave a brief wave to the fairies, but did not stay to introduce themselves.

"The hawk has been here for nearly twenty minutes, waiting to talk to you," Trace told them.

"Hello," said the hawk. His voice was very deep and stern. "Most of the hawks that work on the island do not speak, but I do." His eyes glinted fiercely as he spoke, and the fairies were somewhat alarmed. "Do not be frightened," the hawk said, sensing their apprehension. "I am very glad you have come. Your help will be much appreciated on the island. I will carry you to the Island of Shadows this evening to meet with the King and Queen of Shadowland.

"I can't give you many details of the problem at hand," the hawk continued, "because I don't know very much. I do know that the crisis has something to do with the Demon of Light. You will get more information from the gryphon on the island before you meet with the king and queen. The gryphon works for the King and Queen of Shadowland. He supervises the hawks and is overseer for the shadow deliveries."

Then Trace told the fairies, "I won't be able to accompany you, but I will come back to this stretch of beach in the morning to see you safely home after your mission." With this, the elf simply vanished with a small *pop*.

Next, the hawk informed them, "We should leave right away. The journey will take several hours, so it will be dark by the time we reach the island. I will carry you all on my back. I have carried much heavier things before so don't worry, you will all be safe."

The fairies were very excited as they flew up to land on the hawk's back. None of them had ever ridden on a hawk before. His feathers were soft and warm.

"You can hold tightly to my feathers if you need to," he said. "The wind may be strong as high as we will be flying."

The hawk did indeed soar very high, and he changed course several times. He seemed to be catching certain winds to help with speed on their journey. Even though the air was very cool this high up, the fairies

were nestled deep in the hawk's soft feathers, so they were plenty warm enough.

The glittering blue ocean was far beneath them, and the immense stretch of water was beautiful when the fairies were able to glimpse it through the swirls, puffs, and strings of white clouds.

As they traveled, Cinnabar looked up Demon of Light in her handbook. Again, she read aloud to her friends:

"Demon of Light: Also known as Lambent Blaze, the Demon of Light, like all demons, is intent on causing human suffering and misery. Most demons torment and torture human beings every chance they get. The Demon of Light seeks to rid the earth of all shadows. However, shadow and light must exist in balance with one another. Lambent Blaze has never been able

to harm human shadows. They are too complex, too powerful, and too numerous for the demon to have any affect on them. A chimera works for Lambent Blaze. Working together in the past, these two evil creatures have managed to cause severe sunburn, certain forest fires, solar flares, snow blindness, and some intense volcanic eruptions. They are a very nasty team."

Cinnabar quickly looked up chimera next:

"Chimera: A chimera is an evil, grotesque, fire-breathing monster with the head of a lion, the body of a goat, and the tail of a snake. The Demon of Light has a chimera working for him. Both of them are very dangerous. Be careful."

As the fairies sat thinking about the Demon of Light and the chimera, and dreading the possibility of facing either or both of them, Dewberry interrupted their thoughts. "Well, that's not exactly correct," she said. "A chimera is any creature composed of two or more types of animals, birds, reptiles, etc. While the traditional form of chimera has a lion's head, goat's body, and serpent's tail, we can't know for sure what the Demon of Light's chimera will consist of."

The rest of the fairies all looked at Dewberry admiringly. They knew that her special fairy gift was great knowledge, but they were very impressed that she was able to add something to the handbook's definition. Ordinarily, the fairy handbook was very complete and thorough.

Dewberry continued a moment later, looking very serious and scrunching her eyebrows together. "Of course, I *do* use my handbook sometimes. But I find it to be somewhat limited and often lacking in detail."

She had clearly gone too far with this statement. The other fairies' eyes all widened and their mouths dropped open, and they heard the fairy handbook on Dewberry's belt grumble and say, "*Harrumph!*"

Everyone kept silent. None of the fairies had ever heard of a fairy handbook making noises of any kind. But, then, they had never met a fairy handbook that had just been insulted.

Cinnabar thumbed through her handbook quickly and read out the definition of gryphon next to try to smooth over tensions. It seemed that *her* handbook was a little fearful of being criticized and gave a very detailed definition:

"*Gryphon: A gryphon is a magical creature with the head and wings of an eagle and the body of a lion. It is not entirely clear what magical abilities gryphons possess, other than flight and the gift of speech. The gryphon you are going to meet works for the King and Queen of Shadowland, otherwise known as King Penumbra and Queen Silhouette of the Island of Shadows. The gryphon is in charge of all of the activities of the hawks that work on the island. He supervises their training and the hawks' delivery operations, which involve uniting specific human shadows with new-born children all over the world. Gryphon may be spelled four different ways: g-r-y-p-h-o-n, g-r-i-f-f-o-n, g-r-i-f-f-e-n, and g-r-i-f-f-i-n."*

The group was silent, as everyone waited to see if Dewberry was going to add anything. She didn't speak, but looked out over the ocean pensively.

Gryphon:

A gryphon is a magical creature with the head and wings of an eagle and the body of a lion.

The other fairies all breathed a sigh of relief. Cinnabar might have imagined it, but she thought she heard her handbook give a small sigh, also in relief, as she tucked the book back into her belt.

The wind had become even colder as they traveled, so the fairies snuggled more deeply into the hawk's feathers for the rest of the journey.

After nearly two hours of flight, they ate a light meal of peanut butter and marsh-mallow crème sandwiches and raspberries. Spiderwort offered some to the hawk, but he declined.

The sun was just going down over the watery horizon, and the ocean beneath them became a steely gray, when the Island of Shadows appeared in the distance.

The fairies all whispered, "*Fairy light*," to light their wands for the dark part of the journey. They knew they would have to extinguish their wands just before reaching the island. But for now, the light was some comfort to the girls, with darkness closing in around them and cold wind whistling in their tiny ears.

The only fairy not bothered by the darkness was Cinnabar. As the blackness of night loomed, she felt a burst of energy surge through her, and her senses were very much heightened. She could see the island more clearly now than a few minutes ago, and she could also see several porpoises in the water below that she had not noticed before. They were traveling very fast, almost as though they were trying to keep pace with the soaring hawk. Streaking along and splashing happily, the porpoises danced and dove gracefully, cutting swiftly through the surface waves.

Chapter Five

The Gryphon

The hawk soared very low over the ocean waves, sweeping in slow circles, still a fair distance from the shores of the island. He seemed to be looking for something. After a few moments, he spotted what he was looking for and flew low to a position directly above a large sea turtle.

He spoke to the turtle by means of several short screeches. Then the hawk explained to the fairies, "The turtle is going to take you on her back for the approach to the shore. The starlight is very bright, and we cannot take a chance that your shadows will be visible. They might be if you arrive on a hawk. I will meet you at the shore, where you will take shelter right away under my wings."

The fairies all nodded and extinguished their wands, as they took off from the hawk's back and made their way down to the turtle. As they landed on her back, she slowly began to swim toward the shore. She was careful that the top part of her shell stayed above the surface of the water at all times, so the fairies would not get swept away by waves.

The ride on the sea turtle was pretty choppy, and Mimosa got a little queasy with seasickness. Her skin turned a weird green color, and she moaned, holding her stomach. She was also sweating and breathing very fast.

Madam Finch pointed her tiger whisker wand at Mimosa's stomach and uttered, "*Still,*" to help calm the nausea. The spell

worked. Within a few seconds, Mimosa was no longer green, and she was smiling.

The Island of Shadows was a volcanic island, very bleak and bare, with dark black sand. To the left of the spot where the turtle landed, a grove of leafless, dead-looking trees stood out against the darkness. They had gray and white trunks that glowed softly in the moonlight. Several very large nests, each about four feet across, were visible in the branches of the nearest trees.

When the turtle had made her way several feet ashore, the fairies quickly thanked her and scurried to reach the hawk to take shelter under his outstretched wings. "I will leave you with the gryphon while I inform the king and queen that you are here," said the hawk.

The fairies hadn't even noticed the huge gryphon on the shore, and it was hard to believe they could have missed him. He was a light, golden brown color and was very large—larger than a cow, in fact. His feathers shone brilliantly in the pale moonlight, and his lion's coat looked like a shimmering ripple of liquid gold. The gryphon held out his enormous eagle wing for them, and the fairies walked from under the hawk's wing to under the gryphon's wing. The transfer was a smooth one, and their shadows were never seen.

The hawk flew off as the gryphon began speaking to the fairies. "We are very glad you have come."

The hawk's voice had been deep and stern, but the gryphon's voice was even deeper and more serious. He was not overly loud, but his tone sounded like roaring waves and rumbling thunder. This was the lowest and darkest voice the fairies had ever heard. If voices were assigned a color, the gryphon's would have been blacker than coal. His voice also sounded distant, as though it were coming from a deep cavern or one of the hollow volcanoes on the island.

"I will take you to the king and queen shortly," the gryphon added. "An albatross warned us of your arrival, and the king and queen are making some arrangements to meet with you. Take rest for a few minutes. You may need it later."

The fairies all stayed quiet and looked out at their surroundings. In the distance, they could see several shadowmakers working at long tables. They were larger than elves, but smaller than trolls, which is to say that they were about the size of dwarves, between three and four feet in height.

The shadowmakers all looked as though they were made from glittering sand, in numerous shades of gray. Spiderwort had seen the Sandman before, when he came to their Fairy Circle last year, but he had been made of golden sand. The shadowmakers seemed to be made of many

different colors of sand such as storm cloud, graphite, and elephant gray. One was so light that he looked like pale smoke.

There were fat ones and thin ones, and some in between; and all of them were working furiously. The shadowmakers wore tool belts containing an assortment of odd tools that looked like fancy chisels, needles, hammers, pinchers, measuring cups, snips, rolling pins, and scales. They concentrated on their work very hard, taking no notice of the fairies while they sculpted, pinched, measured, flattened, and wove the intricate shadows.

After about ten minutes, all of the shadowmakers put away their work and slipped off quietly. The fairies assumed it must be time for their break.

Chapter Six

King Penumbra
and Queen Silhouette

As the shadowmakers disappeared into the darkness, the hawk returned and spoke to the gryphon in low tones. Then the gryphon told the fairies. "It is safe for you to come out from under my wing. You may also fly, as long as you stay close to me," he added. "The king and queen have sent the shadowmakers to work on the other side of the island for now, so they are safe from your shadows."

"What about the king and queen?" Cinnabar asked. "Will they be safe from our shadows?" she added, worriedly. The other fairies were also concerned. The last thing any of them wanted to do was cause the death of a shadowmaker, or the king or queen.

"You are very conscientious," said the gryphon, appreciatively. "Yes, they are safe. I will let the king explain the reason to you though. He will be better able to give you that answer himself."

The fairies flew alongside the gryphon, but slightly above his large wings, which generated strong gusts of air with each flap. They flew straight to the top of one of the larger volcanoes. Fortunately, the volcano was not an active one, so it was safe to enter. They followed the gryphon down into the black, craggy opening, past sharp and shining rocks.

A long, spiraling staircase, with thousands of steps, circled the inside walls of the hollow volcano. The fairies were glad

they could fly. Descending by stairs would have taken a very long time.

The king and queen were in a massive chamber very near the bottom of the volcano. The fairies' eyes were used to the darkness by the time they reached the bottom, and they could see fairly well.

King Penumbra and Queen Silhouette were very old shadowmakers. The king was extremely tall and thin, and the queen was somewhat short and pudgy. They sat on giant black thrones made of polished, sculpted obsidian. The large, glassy thrones upon which they sat made the king and queen look rather small.

"Hello, and welcome!" said the king. "We have never had a visit from fairies before. I am glad you are here. I have sent all of the shadowmakers to work on the far side of the island while you are here, so they will be safe from your shadows. You may light your wands if you wish."

Cinnabar looked at Madam Finch first, and received a nod of approval, before she whispered, *"Fairy light."* The tip of her aspen twig wand immediately glowed with a soft light.

The light from only one wand was plenty bright enough, because the rocks inside the volcano sparkled with dazzling warmth. Cinnabar didn't really need the light, but she hoped it would make the other fairies feel better. So far, their journey had been a tense one, traveling in the darkness and meeting unfamiliar creatures like the gryphon.

The gryphon whispered something to the king, who nodded. Then the giant, golden creature settled himself next to the king's throne to listen and await instructions.

Finally, the king spoke again. "Neither the queen nor I have made any shadows for the past seventy-five years, so we could not possibly have made any of your shadows. We are quite safe," he explained.

Madam Goldenrod muttered under her breath, "You cut it a little close with me, since I'm seventy-three." She shook her head slightly and breathed an extra sigh of relief that she was not yet seventy-five and could not endanger the king and queen. Madam Goldenrod knew very well that she looked fairly young, and she doubted that many creatures would guess her age at over sixty.

"Now, let me explain the problem," the king continued. "Twelve shadows that were designated for delivery have been stolen." The fairies all shuddered. They were surprised, and dismayed, to find out that there were more than seven shadows missing. The king spoke sadly. "Unless we locate

the stolen shadows, the newborns they were intended for will not receive them. Disaster will follow, torment and misery for the twelve children, and possibly all of mankind. The shadows cannot be remade. The individual shadow blueprints are only available while the shadows are being constructed.

"We have done some investigating and discovered that a shadowmaker named Lumencast has turned evil. He is working for Lambent Blaze, the Demon of Light. We have Lumencast in custody, but we have been unable to get him to divulge what has happened to the stolen shadows.

"As you may know," the king added, "the Demon of Light seeks to torture mankind by destroying shadows whenever he can. But he has never troubled us on the island before, or directly attacked human shadows, that we know of. This action was very unexpected." The fairies all nodded as the gryphon, sitting beside the king and queen, listened intently.

Suddenly, from very high above, a horrible roaring sound was heard.

Chapter Seven

The Battle

The king and queen looked frightened, and the gryphon magically vanished. This explained why the fairies had not noticed him at first upon their arrival to the island. Apparently, he had the ability to appear and disappear at will, like elves and leprechauns.

Even though this group of fairies was composed mainly of "thinker" fairies, they were still fairies of action with plenty of courage and bravery, and a strong sense of duty. They immediately took off for the mouth of the volcano to find out what was wrong.

As they reached the opening, a very disturbing sight met them. The gryphon was suspended in flight, hovering near the shore. Still over the sea, but moving ever closer, was the chimera. He looked to be floating on a blazing cloud of light shaped like a flat, oval platter that was very bright and almost fiery. The light from the cloud made the rocky beach and the side of the volcano look almost as though they were displayed in daylight.

The handbook had told the fairies that the chimera was a grotesque monster, and it wasn't kidding. This chimera *was* in the traditional form with a lion's head, goat's body, and serpent's tail.

The chimera's head was shaggy with a black mane, and it was oddly oversized for the rest of the creature. The goat part of him was lumpy, with brown and white spots; and his body only had two legs, with huge feet and enormous goat hooves. He also had two tiny arms with hooves that looked as though they couldn't possibly have belonged to such a large creature. The monster's striped, green-and-yellow tail was very thick near the body, but tapered off to a point at the tip. The shape reminded the fairies of a dinosaur's tail. The chimera was so oddly shaped and out of proportion that it seemed the tail was needed to steady the monster on his two feet like a tripod.

"Quick, girls!" said Madam Finch. "Follow our lead, but stay behind us!" she commanded.

Madam Finch and Madam Goldenrod flew down to the beach with Cinnabar, Dewberry, Mimosa, and Spiderwort following closely behind. The fairies stationed themselves behind a large group of rocks along the shore. The gryphon was holding position directly in front of them, about twenty feet high in the air.

As the chimera neared the shore, he jumped off the platter of light, landing with a ground-shaking boom as his giant hooves hit the sand. The monster was more than twice the size of the gryphon.

The chimera let loose another loud, throaty roar, and the sound was horrible. Next, he shot a stream of fire out of his mouth at the gryphon. The gryphon moved very fast, dodging the flames.

Madam Finch and Madam Goldenrod held their wands directly overhead, pointing up, and said, "*Fountain.*" Water immediately spurted out of their wands and formed a protective water umbrella over them. The young fairies all followed suit and were also protected from the chimera's fire.

The chimera continued to roar and shoot fire, and the gryphon continued to evade. He reminded the fairies of their friend, Dragonfly, zooming around. They would never have imagined that a creature the size of the gryphon could move so quickly.

However, the chimera seemed to have endless fire, and the gryphon was tiring. At one point, one of the jets of fire singed the gryphon's back leg, and he was forced to retreat several feet.

Madam Finch and Madam Goldenrod took action to help. Each grabbing a handful of pixie dust out of their pouches, they tossed the magical dust high into the air. Then, pointing their wands, they both shouted, "*Fire!*" Each speck of glittering pixie dust turned into a powerful flying fireball, amounting to hundreds of them, all now sailing directly towards the chimera. However, though he could not fly, the creature was able to move backwards very quickly, so he was able to dodge most of them.

The fireballs that did manage strike the chimera didn't seem to hurt him. They just made him mad. He roared even more loudly and shot fire at the fairies, who again took shelter behind the rocks and under their water-umbrella-fountains.

"I guess we can't fight fire with fire, in this case," said Madam Goldenrod.

After only a brief retreat, the gryphon was back in action. He had had time to regroup and was now shooting strings of what looked like dark shadowy ropes out of his eagle's mouth. The shadow ropes covered the chimera, twisting and tightening around his body, while the monster struggled against the bonds.

The cloud platter of light that the chimera arrived on had begun to take a different shape as it hovered above the writhing monster. The cloud was actually the Demon of Light, and like most demons, Lambent Blaze was able to shift his form into any shape and state he liked. The demon was currently turning into a large, round-shaped creature of light with

long spikes. He flashed and glared brilliantly, and shot out shards of light to sting their eyes. The gryphon and fairies all had to look away from the blinding flashes.

Even in the nighttime, the Demon of Light was an entity very much like the sun, too bright to look at directly. However, there was no warmth from this light. Instead, the area along the shore was freezing cold, as though the island had been hit by an arctic winter blast. The fairies could hardly believe something so bright could be so cold.

Meanwhile, on the beach below the demon, the struggles of the chimera were paying off. He was almost free from his shadow ropes by the time the fairies were able to look again.

"Everyone, move forward," said Madam Finch, determinedly. She pointed her wand in the direction of the chimera and demon, and said, "*Darkness envelop.*"

Sooty gray clouds of vapor immediately began seeping out of her wand, and the dark clouds quickly made their way towards the chimera and Lambent Blaze.

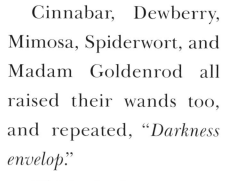

Cinnabar, Dewberry, Mimosa, Spiderwort, and Madam Goldenrod all raised their wands too, and repeated, "*Darkness envelop.*"

Thick shadowy vapors issued from the additional wands and headed toward the demon and chimera.

Suddenly, Madam Goldenrod's hummingbird feather wand seemed to become possessed of a will of its own. The feather flew out of her hand, rising to a position high above the other wands, flitting back and forth, and emitting the dark vapory clouds at a rate ten times that of the other wands. The tiny feather was obviously full of hummingbird enchantment, along with fairy magic, and couldn't help itself.

Soon the chimera and the Demon of Light were completely covered in a blanket of the dark clouds, which wrapped tightly about them, imprisoning them.

Madam Goldenrod's wand came back down to her hand, humming and buzzing happily, as the fairy mentor exclaimed laughingly, "Good job!"

$\mathscr{T}$he $\mathscr{S}$tolen

Shadows

Only the chimera's head was visible, sticking out of the shadowy blanket. The Demon of Light had also formed a head. It too stuck out of the shadows binding him. He had a pointed nose and chin with sharp cheekbones and ugly, glaring orange eyes. Jagged hands and feet also became visible, poking out of the dark shadows. Lambent Blaze had long hands and feet with sharp sparkling claws.

Thank goodness no one had been seriously injured in the battle. The fairies mainly only had a few scrapes and bruises, and the gryphon's burns were not bad.

However, Mimosa was very concerned. She offered to use pixie dust with a *Healing Spell*, but the gryphon shook his head. "Don't worry about me. I heal very quickly," he informed her.

King Penumbra and Queen Silhouette had finally made their way up the winding staircase and down the side of the volcano. They stood with the fairies and gryphon in front of the two captives.

No one spoke for a few moments, then the king said, "They should be killed."

He turned to the gryphon, apparently about to give orders, when Mimosa and Spiderwort shouted, "No!" in unison.

Cinnabar moved closer to the king and told him, "They must live, as part of a necessary balance. Light and shadow must both exist. We couldn't have one without the other."

Madam Finch also stepped forward, in her best negotiating posture, to try to smooth things over and to try to convince the king not to act hastily. "What she says is true. You cannot decide their fate. We should let Mother Nature deal with them."

The king looked at the fairies, then back at the demon and chimera. His eyebrows knitted together while he thought very hard. After a very long pause, he stated, "You are right. Mother Nature should decide their punishment."

King Penumbra was about to add something else when he was interrupted. The Demon of Light had started laughing. The sound was cold and cruel, a harsh sound like huge icicles dropping from a roof and crashing onto hard cement. Then the demon spoke to the group. "I do not answer to Mother Nature. She has no power over me."

Suddenly, a brilliant flash and a terrific crash startled them, as lightning struck a point directly between the chimera and

Lambent Blaze. And far out over the ocean expanse, the fairies spotted a tremendous waterspout, streaking across the water. None of them had ever seen a sea twister before. The huge, watery cyclone reached the shore very quickly. Scooping up the chimera and the demon, the waterspout carried them swiftly away from the island.

No one said anything for a few moments, then the king said, "I'd say Mother Nature *does* have control over the Demon of Light; he just didn't know it."

Madam Finch next addressed the king again. "Please, take us to Lumencast."

Lumencast seemed to know that he was in a lot of trouble, and that the Demon of Light was not coming to help him. As the surly shadowmaker glared at the fairies, he hung his head and kept silent.

Madam Finch took out her tiger whisker wand, but addressed the younger fairies before she used it. "You are never allowed

to use this spell unless a mentor fairy is supervising you, and even then, only under special circumstances. The only reason I am allowed to use this spell today is to ensure the success of our vital mission."

Cinnabar, Mimosa, Spiderwort, and Dewberry all nodded. They already knew this, but it was a mentor's job to remind them, so they didn't mind hearing it.

Madam Finch then sprinkled a fair amount of pixie dust over Lumencast's head, pointed her wand, and uttered, "*Truth.*"

Light streamed from her wand and formed a twinkling, green-and-blue circle that settled on Lumencast's head like a halo. Then Madam Finch asked the shadow-maker, "Where are the stolen shadows?"

The light halo must have been very heavy because Lumencast's head drooped down, like he was folding up, and almost reached his lap.

Unfortunately, the *Truth Spell* wasn't strong enough because Lumencast remained silent. He just continued to glare sideways at them, looking very sullen.

Next, Madam Goldenrod stepped forward. "Everyone leave," she commanded.

The rest of the fairies left the room quickly, without question. They all knew that Madam Goldenrod possessed the power to make others tell the truth. The look on her face at this moment was enough for anyone to fear her fairy gift. And no one wanted to see her in action, not even for a good cause.

She was in the room with the shadow-maker less than two minutes. Lumencast looked unharmed after his encounter with Madam Goldenrod, but his eyes were somewhat glazed over and had an odd vacant look to them.

Madam Goldenrod quickly informed the king and queen, "Search the trees along the Eastern shore of the island. The stolen shadows are concealed in an abandoned hawk's nest."

The gryphon took off at once.

After nearly an hour, he returned, followed by twelve hawks. Each of the hawks carried a tiny, square silver box, about the size of a sugar cube, tied with a midnight-blue ribbon. This was apparently how shadows were packaged for delivery.

"Success!" announced the gryphon. Then he instructed the hawks. "Speed is essential; make as few stops as possible." The hawks each nodded to the gryphon and took off in wide graceful arcs, departing in various directions from the island. In addition to Panama, Canada, South Africa, the Netherlands, Mexico, and the United States, there were also children in Japan, Spain, Belgium, and Norway awaiting the shadows.

The king and queen thanked the fairies for their help. "We could not have done this without you," he said. "We have prepared a small gift for you."

Queen Silhouette presented each of the fairies with a tiny silver shadow box tied with a midnight-blue ribbon. The boxes did not contain shadows since the fairies already had theirs. Instead, they were filled with beautiful, sparkling black sand from the shores of the Island of Shadows.

The sun was just coming up over the horizon as the fairies departed the island. The gryphon himself flew them back to the beach to meet Trace. Their return trip was much quicker since the gryphon could fly faster than a hawk. The golden creature said goodbye to the fairies and thanked them again for their help.

Cinnabar told Trace the details of their adventure. Then the fairies readied themselves for the return trip, taking deep breaths and closing their eyes.

Forty-five minutes later, they woke up under the bald cypress tree in the park where they had held their gathering the day before. Trace had carefully watched over them while they slept. When the fairies were fully awake, the elf said goodbye and disappeared with a small *pop*.

Madam Finch's car and Madam Goldenrod's van were still parked near the pond. Dewberry and Mimosa said goodbye to Cinnabar, Spiderwort, and Madam Finch. Madam Goldenrod would be driving Mimosa to the home of her mentor, Madam Monarch, who had arranged Mimosa's time away from home for the mission under the guise of a two-night sleepover with Marigold, Madam Monarch's niece.

The girls were silent as Madam Finch drove Spiderwort home. Madam Chameleon had arranged Spiderwort's sleepover, but it was only for one night.

Even with the forty-five minute nap, which none of them could remember, the fairies were all very tired and stayed quiet in the car.

The next day, Madam Finch sent nut messages to Madam Toad and several other fairy mentors to inform them of the success of their mission.

Cinnabar sent nut messages to several of her friends as well. She spent a long time composing a message to James, thanking him for the beautiful flower, and telling him about the adventure. A raven was perched on her windowsill, waiting to take the walnut to James.

She also sent a message to Spiderwort to arrange to go skating over the upcoming weekend. Rosemary would be home from her family trip by then, and would be anxious to hear the details of the latest Fairy Circle and their exciting mission. A friendly mockingbird was very happy to take the hazelnut and make the delivery to Spiderwort.

Then Cinnabar composed notes to Periwinkle, Morning Glory, and Primrose to tell them all about the trip to the island and the exciting battle between the chimera and gryphon. After writing for well over an hour, she was ready for a break. A family of squirrels that liked to deliver messages took the three acorns for her.

Cinnabar carefully put the baby's breath flower in her jewelry box for safekeeping. She decided to tie the tiny silver shadow box onto her fairy belt next to her pouch of pixie dust.

Thinking about her latest fairy mission, she went outside and strolled around the sunny back yard for a while, watching her shadow. Since Cinnabar preferred night-time, she had never thought much about her shadow, or the purposes it served. After the trip to the Island of Shadows, she had a whole new appreciation for her constant companion. She was very grateful for

the comfort and protection it provided, and she vowed never to take her shadow for granted.

"It's funny how much alike we are," she said quietly to her shadow. "And when we discuss important things, we never disagree," she added.

After wandering around the back yard for nearly an hour, pondering everything, she whispered a final thought to her shadow. "I think you might be my best friend."

The End

Fairy Fun

My Shadow

by J. H. Sweet

My shadow keeps me company
when I go for walks alone.
Sometimes we discuss important things
and never disagree.
So comforting to find my shadow
walking beside me,
or leading as I follow.
Almost never alone.
But where does my shadow go
when I walk at noon?
To visit other shadows?
Never alone for long.
A few minutes after noon,
my shadow appears behind me,
trying to catch up—to tell me a secret.

Draw a picture of your shadow.
Then write your own poem about it.

Shadow Tracings

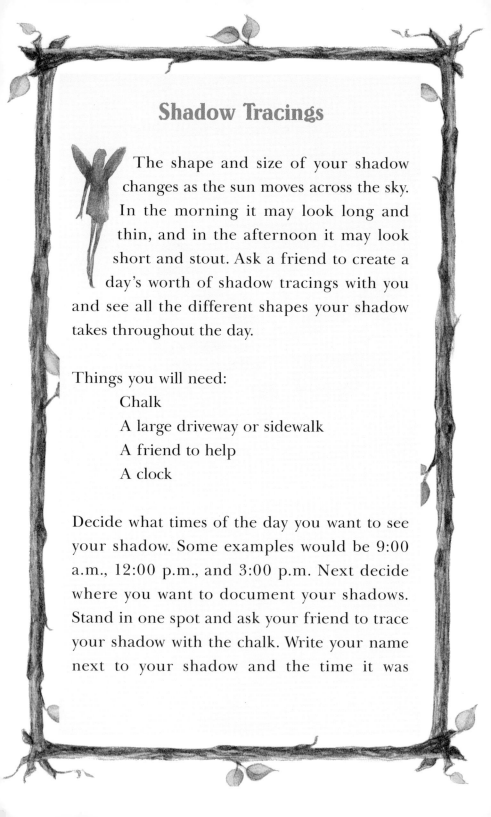

The shape and size of your shadow changes as the sun moves across the sky. In the morning it may look long and thin, and in the afternoon it may look short and stout. Ask a friend to create a day's worth of shadow tracings with you and see all the different shapes your shadow takes throughout the day.

Things you will need:
    Chalk
    A large driveway or sidewalk
    A friend to help
    A clock

Decide what times of the day you want to see your shadow. Some examples would be 9:00 a.m., 12:00 p.m., and 3:00 p.m. Next decide where you want to document your shadows. Stand in one spot and ask your friend to trace your shadow with the chalk. Write your name next to your shadow and the time it was drawn. Now ask your friend to stand still while you trace her shadow on the ground.

Repeat this process as many times as you'd like throughout the day. What happens to your shadow as the sun moves across the sky? What time of day does your shadow look the smallest? What time of day does your shadow look the longest? What time of day makes your favorite shadow shape?

You can also try this experiment indoors on a rainy day! Hang a large piece of paper on a wall. Stand in front of the wall and turn on a bright light in front of you. Ask a friend to trace your shadow on the piece of paper. (Be careful not to write on the wall.) Try standing in different poses and see if your shadow can keep up!

Light and Dark

In the story, the fairies learn that both light and dark must exist for the world to be balanced. Try creating some artwork using only black and white. You can use paint, markers, crayons, or colored pencils. You could even cut up pages from a magazine and make a collage or a mosaic. But limit the colors you use to only black and white.

FAIRY FACTS

Bald Cypress Trees

The bald cypress tree is a conifer and produces cones similar to pinecones, which contain the tree's seeds. Bald cypress trees can grow in many different types of soil and are sometimes even found growing directly in the shallow water of rivers and ponds. When the trees grow in the water, their roots push up out of the water to form shapes that resemble knees. Cypress trees are thought to be trees of shadow and mourning.

Volcanoes

Volcanoes are natural vents that allow gases, ash, and molten rock to escape from within the earth. When too much pressure builds up, an eruption can occur and lava (melted rocks) and gasses shoot up from the ground and through the top of the volcano. When lava flows out of a volcano, it can be as hot as 1,300° to 2,200°F!

There are about 1,500 volcanoes in the world that have erupted over the last 10,000 years. Approximately 50 – 70 volcanoes in the world are still active and erupt each year. Mauna Loa in Hawaii is the earth's largest volcano. At 56,000 feet tall, the volcano covers half of the Island of Hawaii. It has erupted 33 times since 1843. Its last eruption was in 1984.

Inside you is the power to do anything

. . . . the adventures continue

Periwinkle and the Cave of Courage

Fairies always work well together, but what happens when they have to lead a team made up of many different kinds of magical creatures?

"I have been instructed to tell you of a challenge we must all participate in," continued Madam Toad. "Not far from here lies the entrance to the Cave of Courage. The Cave of Courage produces courage for all of mankind. Every one hundred years, the cave must be recharged. This is done by an organized team effort between magical creatures. For this recharging, Mother Nature has chosen a dwarf, a leprechaun, a gnome, a troll, two brownies, and four fairies to participate."

With four fairies involved, no challenge is too difficult, but now they must rely on the help of others, something that not everyone does well...

Come visit us at fairychronicles.com

Mimosa and the River of Wisdom

Mimosa and the River of Wisdom
J. H. SWEET

Life is full of difficult choices. One of the hardest is having the power to help someone you love and not being able to. In such a situation, what would you do?

As they sat on the bed together, Mimosa sighed and tried to word her thoughts carefully. Periwinkle pulled her long dark hair back into a ponytail, clasping it with a stretchy hair tie, as she watched her friend's face closely, waiting for her to speak.

After a few moments, Mimosa sighed again, then finally said, "I'm really worried about my mom. She has tried so hard to quit smoking, but she can't. I want to help her."

"What do you mean, help her?" asked Periwinkle hesitantly.

"Well…" said Mimosa. "You know…a little fairy help."

"But you can't!" Periwinkle cried loudly. She glanced at the door and lowered her voice. "You know that we can't use fairy magic to solve personal problems. You could lose your fairy spirit."

Mimosa is one of the kindest, most courageous fairies in the world. But this is the hardest choice she has ever had to make. Should she use magic to help her mom even if it is forbidden? Should she risk losing her fairy spirit to do this?

Come visit us at fairychronicles.com

113

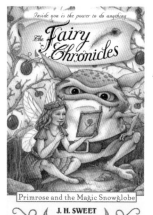

Burchard the gargoyle has just been fired from his job guarding a church from evil spirits because he can't stop walking around, Ripper the gremlin is fixing things instead of breaking them, and Mr. Jones the dwarf is telling people his own name and spreading dwarf secrets to non-dwarves. What is wrong with these people?

When Madam Toad had everyone's attention, she spoke more solemnly. "By now, many of you may have guessed why our visitors are here. It is unusual for a gargoyle to move around, for a gremlin to enjoy fixing things, and for a dwarf to reveal secrets. As far as anyone can tell, these are recent and singular occurrences among gargoyles, gremlins, and dwarves. Burchard has been fired from his job. Ripper has been driven out and is being pursued by other gremlins. And Mr. Jones has been banished by the dwarves.

"We have no idea how these things occurred," Madam Toad continued, "and a reason why must be found so that things can be put to right."

Primrose, Luna, and Snapdragon are put on the case, with the help of Madam Swallowtail. Interestingly, all three of the magical creatures remember making a wish and seeing a man with a snowglobe. Could it really be that the Wishmaker has returned? Primrose must use her detective abilities to solve the mystery.

Come visit us at fairychronicles.com

Luna and the Well of Secrets

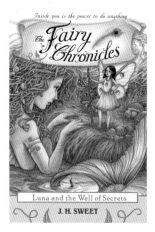

Three bat fairies have been kidnapped and taken to the Well of Secrets. To make matters worse, the Well of Secrets is the doorway to Eventide, the Land of Darkness!

"There must be extremely powerful magic involved to snatch fairies from three completely different parts of the world all in one day."

Madam Toad's face wore a puzzled expression as she continued. "And the reason only bat fairies were abducted is unknown..."

Luna, Snapdragon, Firefly, and Madam Finch are sent to the well to discover why. Once there, they discover a Dark Witch imprisoned in a mirror, only able to come out for twelve minutes every twelve hours. Then a Light Witch arrives and the fairies have to make a choice. Who do they trust? Which one is good and which one is evil? Will they defeat the right witch without destroying the balance between light and dark?

This may be the most dangerous fairy mission ever!

Come visit us at fairychronicles.com

The adventures don't end here!

Come visit us at
www.fairychronicles.com

for even more fairy magic and fun!

- Become a Fairy Chronicles member

- Upload your own fairy drawings

- Read about all of the *Fairy Chronicles* adventures—and get sneak peeks of the next books

- Meet each fairy and learn more about your favorite characters

- Help protect Mother Nature with cool recycling activities and ideas

- Check out the online Fairy Handbook as well as trivia, recipes, poems, and crafts

- Download special bookmarks, computer graphics, and more free stuff

- Send your friends *Fairy Chronicles* e-cards

And much more!

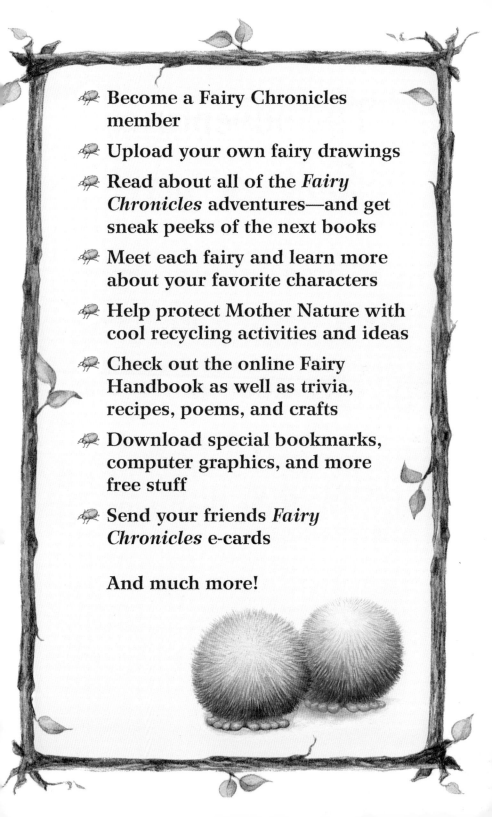

About the Author

J. H. Sweet has always looked for the magic in the everyday. She has an imaginary dog named Jellybean Ebenezer Beast. Her hobbies include hiking, photography, knitting, and basketry. She also enjoys watching a variety of movies and sports. Her favorite superhero is her husband, with Silver Surfer coming in a close second. She loves many of the same things the fairies love, including live oak trees, mockingbirds, weathered terra-cotta, butterflies, bees, and cypress knees. In the fairy game of "If I were a jellybean, what flavor would I be?" she would be green apple. J. H. Sweet lives with her husband in South Texas and has a degree in English from Texas State University.

About the Illustrator

Holly Sierra's illustrations are visually enchanting with particular attention to decorative, mystical, and multicultural themes. Holly received her fine arts education at SUNY Purchase in New York and lives in Myrtle Beach with her husband, Steve, and their three children, Gabrielle, Esme, and Christopher.